lunch

sniff
sniff

This book is for Rochelle

Special thanks to Laura for her patience and
to David and Indigo for their endurance

SQUARE
FISH

An Imprint of Macmillan
175 Fifth Avenue
New York, NY 10010
mackids.com

Square Fish and the Square Fish logo are trademarks of Macmillan and are used by
Henry Holt and Company under license from Macmillan.

Library of Congress Cataloging-in-Publication Data
Fleming, Denise.
Lunch / written and illustrated by Denise Fleming.
p.   cm.
Summary: A very hungry mouse eats a large lunch comprised of colorful foods.
ISBN 978-0-8050-4646-5
[1. Mice—Fiction. 2. Food habits—Fiction. 3. Color—Fiction.] I. Title.
PZ7.F5994Lu 1993   [E]—dc20   92-00178

Originally published in the United States by Henry Holt and Company
First Square Fish Edition: March 2013
Square Fish logo designed by Filomena Tuosto

25 27 29 30 28 26

LEXILE: AD40L

The illustrations were created in handmade paper.

lunch

Denise Fleming

SQUARE
FISH

• Henry Holt and Company • New York

Mouse was _very_ hungry. He was so hungry,

he ate
a crisp
white —

turnip,

tasty
orange —

carrots,

sweet
yellow —

corn,

tender
green —

peas,

tart

blue —

berries,

sour
purple —

grapes,

shiny
red —

apples,

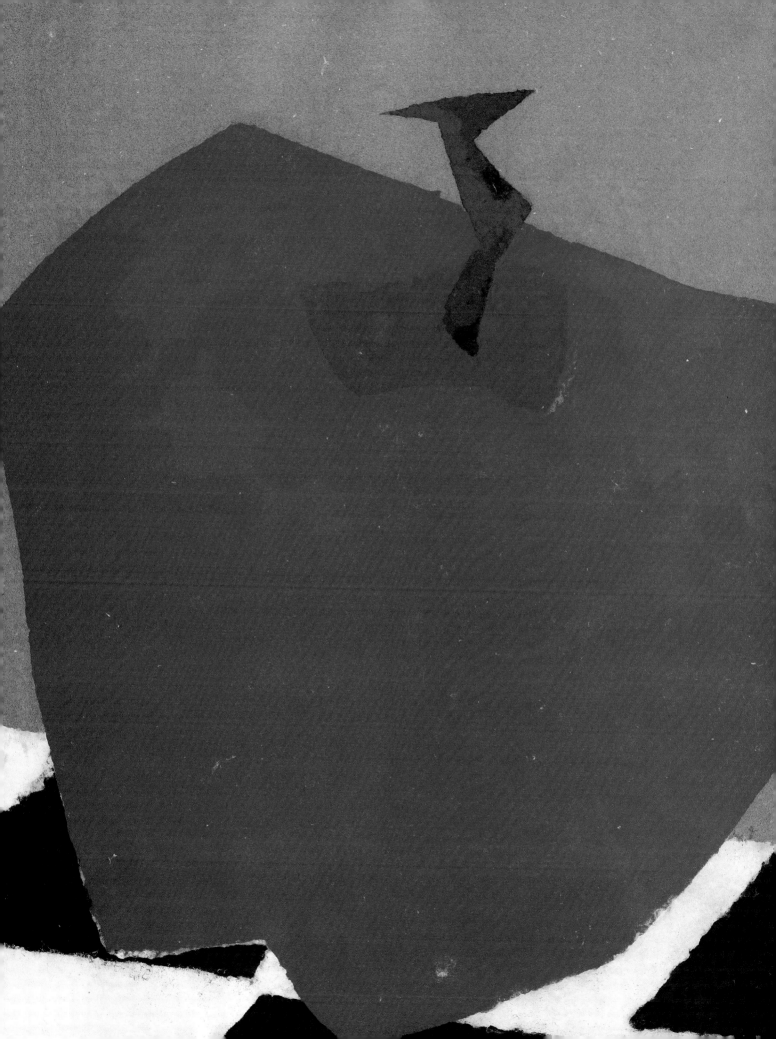

and juicy pink —

watermelon,

crunchy
black seeds
and all.

Then,

he took a nap
until . . .

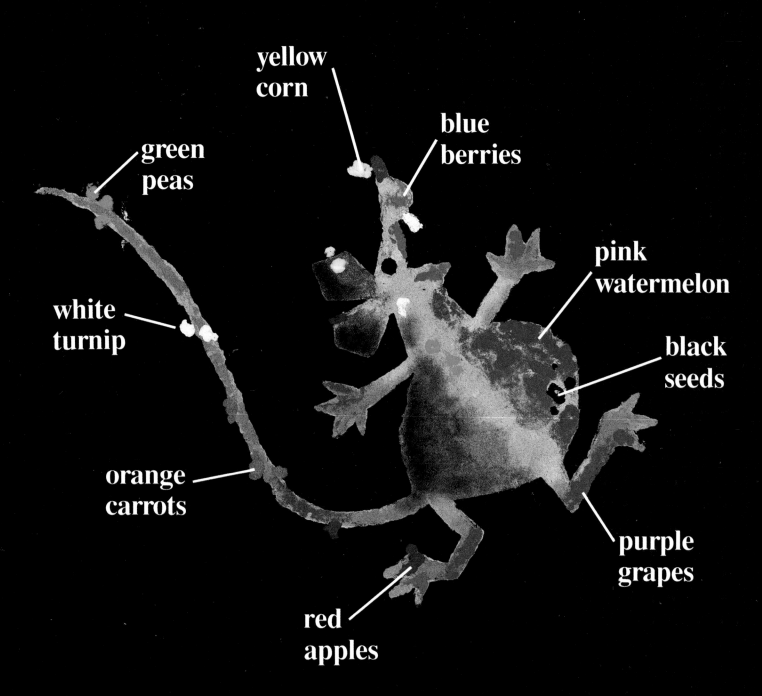

yellow corn

blue berries

green peas

pink watermelon

white turnip

black seeds

orange carrots

purple grapes

red apples